The Monsters on the Bus

By Sarah Albee
Illustrated by Joe Ewers

 A GOLDEN BOOK • NEW YORK

"Sesame Workshop,"® "Sesame Street,"® and associated characters, trademarks, and design elements are owned and licensed by Sesame Workshop. © 2013, 2001 Sesame Workshop. All Rights Reserved. Published in the United States by Golden Books, an imprint of Random House Children's Books, a division of Random House, Inc., 1745 Broadway, New York, NY 10019, and in Canada by Random House of Canada Limited, Toronto, in conjunction with Sesame Workshop. Originally published in 2001 in a different form by Random House Children's Books, a division of Random House, Inc. Golden Books, A Golden Book, A Little Golden Book, the G colophon, and the distinctive gold spine are registered trademarks of Random House, Inc.
randomhouse.com/kids
SesameStreetBooks.com
Educators and librarians, for a variety of teaching tools, visit us at RHTeachersLibrarians.com
ISBN: 978-0-307-98058-8
Library of Congress Control Number: 2012930224

Printed in the United States of America
10 9 8 7 6 5 4 3 2
Random House Children's Books supports the First Amendment and celebrates the right to read.

The wheels on the bus go
round and round,
round and round,
round and round.

The wheels on the bus go
round and round,
all through the town.

The baby on the bus cries,
  "Waah-waah-waah!
  Waah-waah-waah!
  Waah-waah-waah!"

The baby on the bus cries,
  "Waah-waah-waah!"
all through the town.

The parents on the bus say,
  "Shhh-shhh-shhh,
  shhh-shhh-shhh,
  shhh-shhh-shhh."

The parents on the bus say,
  "Shhh-shhh-shhh,"
all through the town.

What a cute baby.

The wipers on the bus go
swish, swish, swish,
all through the town.

A monster on the bus says,
"Coo-ooo-kies!"
all through the town.

The radio on the bus goes
Boom! Boom! Sha-boom!
Boom! Boom! Sha-boom!
Boom! Boom! Sha-boom!

The radio on the bus goes
Boom! Boom! Sha-boom!
all through the town.

The frogs on the bus hop
up and down,
all through the town.

The cows on the bus go,
Moo-oo-oo!
Moo-oo-oo!
Moo-oo-oo!

The grouches on the bus go
Bam! Bam! Bam!
Bam! Bam! Bam!
Bam! Bam! Bam!

The grouches on the bus go
Bam! Bam! Bam!
all through the town.

The band on the bus plays
Oom-pah-pah!
Oom-pah-pah!
Oom-pah-pah!

The Martians on the bus go,
"Yip! Yip! Yip!
Yip! Yip! Yip!
Yip! Yip! Yip!"

The Martians on the bus go,
"Yip! Yip! Yip!"
all through the town.

The bird on the bus sings,
"La! La! La!
La! La! La!
La! La! La!"

The monsters on the bus all
    wave good-bye,
    wave good-bye,
    wave good-bye.

TAXI!!!!!

The monsters on the bus all
    wave good-bye,
all through the town.